BOOK 2

Fairy Blossoms

Poppy and the Vanishing Fairy

By Suzanne Williams
Illustrated by Fiona Sansom

HARPERTROPHY®
AN IMPRINT OF HARPERCOLLINS*PUBLISHERS*

Library of Congress Cataloging-in-Publication Data is available.
ISBN 978-0-06-113940-6

Typography by Andrea Vandergrift

v

First Edition

*To Margaret Miller and Rachel Orr Chan,
with many thanks for your wonderful
contributions to this story and many others*

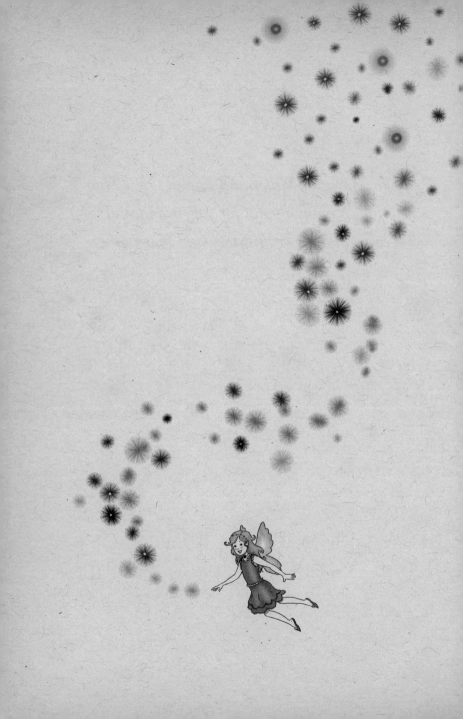

Contents

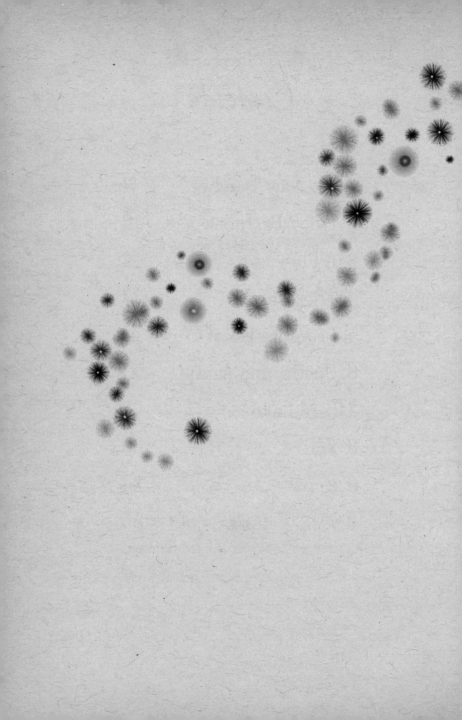

The New Teacher

Fluttering her wings, Poppy flew up to the balcony inside Cloverleaf Cottage and settled at her desk beside her best friend, Daisy. "Have you seen her yet?" Poppy asked. Their teacher, Mistress Lily, was gone for a day, and everyone was curious to meet the substitute teacher.

Before Daisy could reply, a tall fairy with a long, thin nose strode to the front of the

classroom. Her black hair was streaked with gray, and she wore a long, black dress. She leaned against the balcony railing and eyed all eight junior fairies. "I'm Mistress Petunia," she said. "I'll be your teacher today."

"She looks more like a *witch* than a fairy," Poppy whispered in Daisy's ear. "I wonder where she keeps her pointed black hat."

Mistress Petunia scowled at Poppy. "I should tell you that my hearing is excellent."

Poppy gulped. The new teacher might have good hearing, but it didn't sound like she had much of a sense of humor. Mistress Lily, on the other hand, was as good-natured as she was beautiful. She *laughed* at the things Poppy said.

"We'll begin a unit on dressmaking today," said Mistress Petunia. "You'll be designing ball gowns."

An excited hum ran through the classroom.

"Oh, goody!" exclaimed Marigold. A plump fairy with a round face and curly hair, Marigold liked to decorate her wings to go with her outfits. Today her wings shimmered with glittery gold stars that matched the color of her hair and her sparkly gold dress. Poppy had a feeling Marigold would be really good at dressmaking.

Mistress Petunia passed out pictures of dresses. "You can copy one of these designs if you wish, or use your own ideas. Make the gowns to fit yourselves. We don't have space for human-size gowns."

Daisy tugged at one of her thick blond pigtails. "Oh dear," she whispered to Poppy. "I'm not very good at gowns." She was wearing her favorite outfit: a white skirt with a curling zigzag hem and a sleeveless yellow top that ended in points resembling flower petals. She also wore golden shoes with ankle straps.

4

"How hard can they be?" said Poppy. She was wearing her favorite outfit too: a sleeveless green dress with touches of white lace and a scalloped hem, and pointed green dance slippers with poppies on the toes. Pixies love the color green, and Poppy was half pixie. All fairy helpers needed to be good at gown making. It was something they did a lot of.

"Please take out your wands," Mistress Petunia said, "and remember to use small movements."

Poppy ran a finger over her wand. It was gold and sparkled with emeralds She and Daisy looked through their pictures. Poppy held up a photo of a simple, but elegant, sleeveless dress. "I like this one."

"Cute," said Daisy. She showed Poppy a picture of a dress with puffy sleeves, a flowing skirt, and a belt.

"Nice," said Poppy. "Looks difficult, though."

Daisy nodded. "I'll try it anyway."

The two friends started on their dresses. Right away Poppy's wand slipped through her fingers and clattered to the floor. Mistress Petunia looked up from a fairy magazine and glared at her. Poppy took a deep breath and tried again. Finally she was able to whip up some fabric.

"What a lovely shade of green!" Daisy exclaimed.

Poppy frowned. "I was trying to make *yellow*."

"Oh well," said Daisy. "Green's your favorite color, right?"

"True," said Poppy. "But what if the human I'm helping doesn't want a green dress?"

"I see what you mean," said Daisy. The

fabric *she* had created was a beautiful, shiny blue.

Poppy started on the top half of her gown. Everything was going fine, until she flicked her wand too wildly. "Jumping juniper!" she cried as the neck of her dress grew wider and wider. It took her several tries to shrink the neck and finish the dress. Unfortunately, it didn't look much like the one in the picture. Still, it would do.

"How's your dress going?" she asked Daisy.

"You almost done?"

"I just need to fix the belt," Daisy said. "It's too short."

Poppy watched as Daisy flicked her diamond-studded silver wand. Instantly, Daisy's belt snaked across her desk, looped over the balcony railing, and dangled to the main floor. "Oh dear," said Daisy.

"I'll help," said Poppy. Using both their wands, they managed to shrink the belt until it was just the right size. Dressmaking was harder than Poppy had thought it would be!

At the back of the room, three fairies wearing identical sparkly silver dresses and lavender capes were having an argument. Heather, Hyacinth, and Holly were sisters—*triplets*.

"Let's use an alphabet print," Heather said.

Hyacinth shook her fair head. "No, a bunny print."

"Everyone does bunnies!" complained Holly. "Let's do teddy bears."

Poppy grinned. No one but the triplets would use *any* of those prints for a ball gown. But the sisters were totally baby crazy.

Just before the end of class, Mistress Petunia put down her magazine to check on everyone's progress. "Violet," she said, stopping next to a wispy thin fairy with large brown eyes. "Gray *can* be a nice color, but that particular shade is dull. It won't help a young woman attract the attention of a prince—or anyone else, for that matter."

That was probably the point, thought Poppy. Violet was shy. She didn't *like* attention.

Mistress Petunia moved on to the triplets. "The outfits you've created are certainly original," she said. "Only I can't think of any young woman who would want to show up at a ball wearing snap-up sleeper pajamas."

Poppy and Daisy covered their mouths to keep from laughing, but they couldn't help giggling just a little.

"Uh-oh," Daisy whispered a moment later. "Mistress Petunia is coming our way."

The teacher looked at Daisy's dress first. "Hmm," she said. "A rather difficult pattern.

Nice color, though."

Poppy held her breath as Mistress Petunia turned to *her* dress. The teacher shrugged. "Not bad," she said, "for a first try."

It wasn't much of a compliment, thought Poppy. Mistress Lily would have been kinder.

Mistress Petunia saved her praise for Rose's and Marigold's gowns. "Excellent designs and beautifully done," she said. She invited everyone to have a look.

Rose fluttered her glittery pink wings as she showed off her beaded gown of salmon pink satin with its matching fringed shawl. Rose was the most elegant of the eight junior fairies. Her jet-black hair hung in ringlets beneath a silver tiara, and her shoes were tiny pink heels with diagonal straps.

"Gorgeous gown!" Daisy exclaimed.

Poppy only shrugged. The dress *was*

11

gorgeous, but she felt too jealous to say so. She couldn't help it—Rose seemed to be good at everything!

Marigold's dress was very different from Rose's but every bit as wonderful. Hers was made from a light, gauzy fabric that shimmered with all the colors of the rainbow.

"Amazing!" said Poppy.

Soon afterward, Mistress Petunia dismissed the class.

"Will Mistress Lily be back this evening?" Poppy asked as the fairies were leaving.

Mistress Petunia frowned. "What am I now—a fortune-teller?" she said.

Poppy groaned. Mistress Lily couldn't return soon enough!

2

Fairy Fashions

"Have you heard the news?" Daisy exclaimed when Poppy joined her at breakfast the next morning. The junior fairies ate at a long table on the main floor of the cottage. Above the table hung a chandelier with dangling crystals that tinkled like bells whenever a breeze stirred.

Poppy sat next to Daisy on a toadstool

13

draped with a square of tasseled satin cloth. "Is Mistress Lily here?"

Daisy frowned. "That's just it. She hasn't shown up."

"Petal rot!" said Poppy. She reached across the lacy white tablecloth for a poppy-seed muffin.

The junior fairies buzzed with talk of Mistress Lily's absence all through breakfast. They were still discussing it when they flew up to the classroom and sat down.

Mistress Petunia frowned. "Quiet, everyone!"

Poppy and Rose raised their hands at the same time, but Mistress Petunia called on Rose. "Teacher's pet," Poppy muttered under her breath.

"Where's Mistress Lily?" Rose asked.

That was what Poppy had planned to ask!

"I wish I knew," Mistress Petunia grumbled.

"She attended the Fairy Education Board meeting yesterday and should have been back last night. Obviously, she's late. Now please take out your wands. You can keep working on yesterday's gowns."

Marigold raised her hand. "But we've finished our gowns. Should we start on new ones?"

"No," said Mistress Petunia. "No new projects."

"Then what should we do?" Poppy asked.

Mistress Petunia looked at her sternly. "Most of your gowns could be improved. Try straightening seams and hems or adding a ruffle."

Humpf, thought Poppy. She'd rather work on a new dress than have to keep fiddling with the one she had already made.

Rose raised her hand again. "Why don't we model the gowns we made yesterday? We could put on a fashion show!"

For the first time, Mistress Petunia smiled. "Excellent idea! I'll give you all day to plan your show. Then tomorrow you can model your dresses for Mistress Lily."

A bubble of jealousy burst inside Poppy. Rose's idea wasn't *that* great. As the junior fairies retrieved their gowns, Mistress Petunia announced, "I have some work to do in Mistress Lily's office. Rose, you can be in charge of the show."

"Big surprise," Poppy muttered.

Daisy raised an eyebrow. "Well, it *was* her idea."

Shame warmed Poppy's cheeks. "Yes, of course." She slipped on the gown she'd made yesterday.

"That looks really cute on you," said Daisy.

"Thanks," said Poppy.

The top was a little big, but otherwise it fit

well. Poppy made a few careful changes to fix the top. Then she helped Daisy take in the waist on *her* dress and straighten the hem. "How do I look?" Daisy asked, trying it on. "Are the sleeves too puffy?"

Poppy cocked her head. "Not really."

Anyone else wearing the dress might've looked like she was balancing twin blueberries on top of her shoulders. But the puffy blue sleeves seemed to suit Daisy. "You look *fabulous*," said Poppy.

Daisy blushed. "Thank you."

Rose clapped her hands together for attention. "How's everyone doing?" she asked. "Does anyone need help?"

Poppy tried not to feel pleased when no one said that she did.

Show practice began after lunch. Poppy wasn't really interested in modeling, and it wasn't just because the show was Rose's idea. Poppy had *never* enjoyed dressing-up games. Back home, she and her brothers had mostly played outside together—riding horses and camping out under the stars.

So, while the other fairies practiced walking across the room—turning this way

and that to show off their dresses—Poppy
flipped through a book she'd hidden inside a
fashion magazine.

Daisy saw what Poppy was doing and
grinned. "What's your book about?"

"Water fairies," said Poppy. She loved learning about different kinds of fairies, especially those who could shape-shift. Because she was half pixie, she could do that too.

"Do you mean mermaids?" Daisy asked.

"Well, they're one kind of water fairy," Poppy explained, "but sea nymphs and sirens are water fairies too." She shuddered. "And then there are *kelpies*, who are quite charming and musical. But when they take the form of a white horse—"

"Where's Violet?" Rose interrupted in a loud voice.

The fairies all looked around the room, but Violet seemed to have vanished.

3

A Plan

"Come on, Violet," coaxed Holly. "We know you're here somewhere." Violet was the only one of the eight junior fairies who knew how to become invisible.

"I don't want to be in the show!" a voice cried out. "I don't like being watched!"

Poppy didn't really want to be in the show either, but not because she cared if anyone watched her.

"Do it for Mistress Lily, okay?" said Heather.

There was a pause. Then the voice said, "Oh, all right." Seconds later, in a burst of gold glitter, Violet reappeared in a chocolate-colored dress with a lacy collar and fringed hem.

"What a lovely gown," said Rose. "Would you like to model for us right now?"

"Not really," said Violet. But, keeping her eyes on the floor, she walked toward the other fairies. Then she turned in a stiff circle, her arms straight at her sides.

Rose gave her a thumbs-up. "Good job!"

Poppy and Daisy flew outside during the half-hour break between afternoon classes. The triplets were sitting on the jeweled bridge that crossed over the stream in front of the cottage. Poppy and Daisy joined them.

"We think we know why Mistress Lily

hasn't returned," said Heather. Her sisters giggled.

"Oh?" Poppy raised an eyebrow.

Holly tucked a sprig of baby's breath flowers back into the braid pinned across the top of her head. "It's only a guess, really," she said.

Hyacinth sighed. "Wouldn't it be wonderful if we were right?"

"So what do you think happened?" asked Poppy.

Heather hugged herself. "We think she met a handsome male fairy and got swept off her feet!"

"I see," said Poppy. "And she hasn't returned because . . ."

". . . because she's getting married!" the triplets shouted out together.

Holly's eyes lit up. "And after a while she'll probably have a *baby*!"

"Interesting idea," Poppy said carefully.
"But don't you think Mistress Lily would let
us know if she wasn't coming back—even if
she's fallen in love?"

Hyacinth shrugged. "Sure."

"Maybe she sent a letter—only it got lost," suggested Heather.

"Hmm," said Poppy. "You could be right." Mistress Lily was *responsible*. If her return was delayed, of course she'd try to let Mistress Petunia know!

When the last class of the day started, Mistress Lily still wasn't back. "Maybe we should organize a search," Poppy suggested. "What if there's been an accident or she's in some kind of danger?"

"Tut-tut," said Mistress Petunia. "Lily can take care of herself. She just doesn't *want* to come back, that's all. She doesn't even care that I might have plans!"

The junior fairies stared at their substitute. Of course Mistress Lily wanted to come back. She loved teaching! Her eyes twinkled with joy when the fairies mastered their lessons, and she always listened with interest to whatever they had to say.

"Continue to work on your show," Mistress Petunia said. "If you need me, I'll be in Mistress Lily's office."

After she left, everyone looked glum. "Okay," Rose said without much enthusiasm. "Let's put on our gowns and—"

"Hold on," Poppy interrupted. "What if Mistress Petunia is wrong? I think we should try to find out what's happened to Mistress Lily."

"But what about our show?" Marigold asked, glancing at Rose.

"Poppy's right," Rose said, much to Poppy's surprise. "The sooner we find Mistress Lily, the better."

The fairies decided to start with a search of Mistress Lily's office. If there *was* a lost letter, maybe they could find it.

"We'll need a key," said Rose. "Mistress

Petunia always locks the door."

Everyone's face fell.

Poppy thought for a moment. Then she snapped her fingers. "I can get us in *without* a key!"

The other fairies stared at her. "How?" asked Marigold.

"Just leave that to me," said Poppy. "Now, how can we keep Mistress Petunia busy while we're searching the office?"

Holly looked at her sisters. "We can do it."

"Sure," said Heather. "We'll say we need her advice."

"We can ask about the best blessings for newborn babies!" Hyacinth exclaimed.

Poppy sighed. "All right. But we'll need at least twenty minutes for our search."

The triplets nodded.

"Let's post a guard outside the office while we search," said Rose. "Just in case."

"Bink will do it," said Daisy. Bink was a type of fairy called a brownie. He served the fairies their meals and took care of the three winged ponies in the stable behind the cottage. The fairies explained their plan to him during dinner.

Bink pushed back a lock of reddish brown hair that had fallen over one eye. "I'll do it," he said. "I'll come up to the balcony as soon as I finish my chores."

After dinner the triplets found Mistress Petunia and asked her to advise them about baby blessings. "Certainly," she said. She sounded pleased to be asked. That made Poppy feel a little guilty, knowing what they were about to do.

Mistress Petunia and the triplets settled cozily against thistledown cushions on the cottage's main floor. Meanwhile, Poppy, Daisy, Rose, Marigold, and Violet flew over the balcony to the office at the back of the classroom.

"Shouldn't we wait for Bink?" Marigold asked worriedly.

"He'll be here soon," said Poppy. "Let's get started."

The door was locked, just as Rose had said it would be. "So how do we get in?" she asked Poppy.

"Easy. Watch me." Poppy squeezed her eyes shut and focused her mind. A soft roar, like the sound of a seashell held to one's ear, rushed through her brain. Her body tingled all over. Then, with a gentle *pop*, the tingling stopped. Opening her eyes, Poppy examined herself, lifting her six legs one at a time.

From high above, Violet's voice boomed out. "Where did you go, Poppy? Are you invisible?"

"Not at all!" she cried in a tiny voice. "Look down!"

4

The Search

The fairies stared in astonishment at the tiny green beetle on the floor. Raising one of its legs, the beetle waved at them.

"Poppy?" asked Daisy. "Is that you?"

"Yup!" Poppy had to shout to make herself heard. "I shape-shifted! Hold on a second. I'll open the door from the inside." With that, she scuttled under the office door. It swung open moments later. Poppy—back in fairy form now—grinned. "Come on in."

After everyone was inside, Poppy closed the door and relocked it. The fairies stared around them. Mountains of glossy fairy magazines covered the desk and spilled onto the floor.

Rose frowned. "How could anyone make such a big mess in so short a time? Mistress Lily wouldn't leave things this way."

Poppy snorted. "I guess that's why Mistress Petunia keeps the door locked!"

"Let's hope she cleans up before Mistress Lily gets back," said Marigold.

Rose moved a plate of half-eaten fairy cakes off a chair and sat down at the desk. "Shall we divide up the room for our search?" she suggested.

"Sure," said Poppy, wishing she'd said it first. After all, checking the office had been *her* idea.

As Rose and Marigold searched through the desk, Violet took a book from a shelf. She shook out the pages. "We're looking for a letter, right?"

Poppy nodded. "Or maybe a card." As she and Daisy shuffled through the papers, magazines, and books on the floor, Poppy's heart beat fast. What if the triplets couldn't keep Mistress Petunia downstairs? Getting caught was too horrible even to think about!

Suddenly, there was a knock at the door. Poppy jumped so high she had to flutter her wings to reach the floor.

"Are you in there?" Bink asked.

"Yes!" Poppy called back.

"All right," said Bink. "Just wanted to let you know I was here."

He must have climbed the rope ladder at the far end of the balcony, thought Poppy. Brownies couldn't fly. They had no wings. "Thanks," she said. She felt better now that Bink had arrived. He'd find a way to delay Mistress Petunia if the triplets couldn't.

The fairies searched for about twenty

minutes without finding anything. They were about to give up when Poppy pounced on a postcard sandwiched between two magazines. "I found something!" she shouted, waving the card in the air.

"Is it from Mistress Lily?" asked Daisy.

"Yes," said Poppy. "It was sent from the Primrose Hotel. I know where that is. My

family went there on vacation last summer."
Poppy read the card out loud.

> Dear Petunia,
> Thanks for taking over my classes. I hated having to leave, but my meeting should only take a day. Enjoy my students!
> Best wishes,
> Lily

"That sounds like an old message," said Rose.

Poppy sighed. There was no date on the card to tell when it was written, but she was sure Rose was right.

"Sh!" Daisy jerked her head toward the door. "I hear someone! It's Mistress Petunia!"

Everyone froze. Poppy's heart leaped into

her throat. "Aren't you a servant?" she heard Mistress Petunia ask. "What are you doing up here?"

"I . . . um . . . came looking for you," Bink replied. "I wondered if you could check on the ponies."

Good old Bink, thought Poppy.

"Is something the matter with them?" asked Mistress Petunia.

"Perhaps," said Bink. "They're not . . . um . . . eating well."

"I don't know much about ponies," said Mistress Petunia. "I'll look at them later."

Poppy held her breath as the teacher's footsteps came closer. Then she heard the jingle of keys. The five fairies huddled together in a corner.

"No!" Bink exclaimed. "You should come see the ponies *now*."

Mistress Petunia sighed. "Fine," she said, sounding annoyed. "But I want to get something first."

A key turned in the lock, and the fairies gasped as the door swung open.

5

Primrose Hotel

Mistress Petunia stepped inside the office; but to Poppy's surprise, she looked right through the fairies. Why didn't she see them? Poppy wondered. Then she saw the look of concentration on Violet's face. She had cast an invisibility spell over the whole group. Though they could still see one another, Mistress Petunia couldn't see them!

The teacher pulled open a desk drawer and rummaged around in it. From the doorway, Bink glanced around the room. A puzzled smile appeared on his face.

Mistress Petunia opened another drawer. "Where could I have put it?" she said. "Aha! There it is!" She pulled out a colorful brochure and shook it open. Printed in large, sparkly letters were the words *Fairyland Paradise Resort: Where You Don't Need Magic to Make Dreams Come True.* Beneath the words was a picture of several smiling and elegantly dressed fairies dancing in a field of flowers.

With a huge sigh, Mistress Petunia folded the brochure again and stuffed it into her pocket. Then she left the office with Bink, locking the door behind her.

The fairies waited a few minutes to make sure Mistress Petunia wouldn't return. Then Violet made them visible again. Everyone

thanked her. "That was *so* close," said Poppy. "If it wasn't for you, Violet, we would have been caught!"

The fairies searched for a while longer, but without any luck. "I wonder why Mistress

Petunia was looking at that brochure," Poppy said, as they finally left the office.

"She probably wants to go there," said Rose. "Remember her outburst this morning? I bet she had plans to go on vacation as soon as Mistress Lily returned."

The triplets soon joined them on the balcony. "What happened?" asked Heather. "We saw Mistress Petunia go outside with Bink."

"We kept her as long as we could," Holly said.

"It's okay," said Poppy. "She came into the office, but she didn't see us—thanks to Violet's invisibility spell."

"Phew," said Hyacinth. "Did you find any letters?"

"A postcard," said Daisy. "But it was an old one."

"From the Primrose Hotel," said Poppy.

"That's where she went."

"How long would it take to get there?" asked Rose.

Poppy thought for a moment. "Five hours. Maybe three on the winged ponies."

"But what if Mistress Lily isn't there?" asked Marigold.

"Then someone at the hotel might know where she went," said Poppy. "Mistress Petunia might let some of us go. After all, the sooner we find Mistress Lily, the sooner *she* can join in the dancing at the Fairyland Paradise Resort!"

"Huh?" chorused the triplets.

"She wants to go there on vacation," Daisy explained.

The fairies talked awhile longer. Then Poppy volunteered to ask permission to search for Mistress Lily.

"I'll come with you," said Rose.

"All right," Poppy agreed reluctantly. If Rose asked, Mistress Petunia might be more likely to say yes.

The two fairies caught Mistress Petunia on her return from the stable. "We want to search for Mistress Lily," said Rose. "All of the junior fairies do. We want to fly to the Primrose Hotel."

Mistress Petunia sighed. "She's not there. I already checked."

"She might have told someone there where she was going," said Poppy. "We could ask around."

"We'd hate for you to give up your vacation plans," Rose said sweetly.

Mistress Petunia arched an eyebrow. "What do *you* know about my plans?"

"You . . . uh . . . mentioned that you had some," Rose said quickly.

"Oh," said Mistress Petunia. "I suppose I did." She put her hand in her pocket as if to check for the brochure.

"If we borrowed the ponies, we could travel faster," Poppy said.

Mistress Petunia shook her head. "They

could be ill. Bink says they're not eating properly."

Poppy and Rose traded secret smiles. "Could we take them if Bink says they're well enough to travel?" asked Poppy. Mistress Lily had taken one of the three ponies when she left, but the junior fairies could double up on the other two ponies.

Mistress Petunia thought for a moment. Finally she said, "All right. If Lily's not back by tomorrow morning, you can go then. But just you two—I can't let everyone leave."

Poppy's heart sank. She'd rather go with *Daisy* than Rose! But if she made a fuss, Mistress Petunia might decide that *nobody* could go.

"Fly straight to the hotel," said Mistress Petunia. "No stopping along the way. And I don't want you flying after dark. You can spend the night at the hotel and return the next day."

"All right," Poppy and Rose agreed.

"By the way," said Mistress Petunia, "how did you know that Mistress Lily was staying at the Primrose Hotel? I don't believe I told you that."

"Isn't that where the Fairy Education Board always meets?" Rose asked innocently.

"I don't know," Mistress Petunia admitted. "Maybe you're right."

"Phew," Rose said as she and Poppy flew off to find the other fairies.

Though Poppy was disappointed that Daisy wouldn't be coming with her, she grinned. "You can say that again."

6

Up, Up, and Away!

By morning Mistress Lily had still not returned. So after breakfast Poppy and Rose met at the stable. Their ponies were ready to go, with fresh flowers and new ribbons wound through their manes and tails.

Poppy climbed onto Jade. The light green pony was her favorite. Rose settled on top of Opal, a milky white pony covered with pastel specks of pink, blue, and green.

As soon as the two fairies were seated, the ponies took off. Flapping their wings, they galloped a few paces, then rose into the air.

"Head past the village!" Poppy shouted.

The ponies skimmed over the clover-covered cottage and the jeweled golden bridge that crossed the stream at the foot of the lawn. Then they rose higher, sailing above a path bordered with pink clover blossoms, past the fairy houses and shops of Cloverleaf Village.

After leaving the village, the ponies turned west. They flew steadily on for three hours, past forests and hills and meadows. At long last, Poppy recognized a clearing. "It's down there," she called out.

The Primrose Hotel was an old-fashioned place, with narrow windows and a wide,

covered porch. The ponies landed near a
cobbled walkway bordered by dozens of
primroses. Leaving the ponies outside, Poppy

and Rose flew across the porch and entered the hotel.

They went up to the front desk. "We're trying to find someone," Poppy said to the fairy clerk on duty. "Her name is Mistress . . . I mean, *Lily*."

"She was here for the Fairy Education Board meetings," Rose added.

"I'm sorry, but those guests left two nights ago," said the clerk.

"Do you know where she might have gone afterward?" asked Poppy. "We're from Cloverleaf Cottage. She's our teacher there."

"I wish I could help you," said the clerk. "What does she look like, your missing teacher?"

"She has long golden hair and she's very beautiful," said Poppy.

The fairy clerk smiled. "Most fairies are

beautiful, but I think I remember her. She caught the eye of a male fairy who dines here often. He wasn't staying at the hotel, though." She paused. "I saw them having dinner together."

"You don't think she's with him now, do you?" asked Poppy. What if the triplets were right? What if Mistress Lily had fallen in love, gotten married, and decided not to teach anymore? Would they be stuck with Mistress Petunia forever?

"I couldn't say." The clerk's eyes turned dreamy. "He was awfully handsome, with long blond hair, and eyes the blue-green color of the sea. Charming, too. And he had a wonderful voice. I heard him singing one night."

Rose leaned over the desk. "Do you remember his name?"

"Kell," she said with a sigh.

"Do you know where we can find him?" asked Poppy.

"I heard he lives near a lake," the clerk said. "Could be Fern Lake. That's the closest one around. It's just north of here."

"Thanks for your help," said Poppy. The fairies turned to leave.

"Good luck!" called the clerk. "I hope you

find your teacher!"

Poppy hoped so too. But what if they did, and Mistress Lily didn't want to come back?

It was easy to spot Fern Lake from the air. Once the ponies landed, Poppy asked the first fairy they met where Kell lived. The fairy gave

them a funny look, but she directed them to a little wooden house right next to the lake.

When they stood before the door, Poppy knocked. Then she crossed her fingers and wished hard for Mistress Lily to appear.

7

Fern Lake

*P*oppy and Rose waited on the doorstep a long time. At last Poppy said with a sigh, "Nobody's home." But just then she heard a familiar voice behind them!

Poppy jumped in surprise as Mistress Lily exclaimed, "What are *you* doing here?" Beside her stood Ruby, the winged pony that Mistress Lily had ridden on her trip.

"We came to find you," said Rose.

Mistress Lily wrinkled her forehead. "Find me?" she repeated. "I don't understand." She patted the pink pony.

Poppy couldn't believe it. Mistress Lily was acting like nothing was the matter. Heat rose in Poppy's cheeks. "Nobody knew where you were!" she exclaimed. "You were only supposed to be gone for a day!"

Mistress Lily's blue eyes held a look of confusion. She fingered the sapphire necklace that hung at her throat. "But I don't teach at Cloverleaf Cottage anymore," she said in a faraway voice.

"What do you mean?" asked Rose. "Of course you do!"

Cold fear gripped Poppy's stomach. Had Mistress Lily *quit* teaching?

"I don't teach at Cloverleaf Cottage," Mistress Lily repeated dreamily. There was a glazed look in her eyes. Was there something wrong with Mistress Lily? Poppy wondered.

Speaking slowly, as if to a child, she said, "Mistress Petunia is waiting for you to return so she can go on vacation."

"Won't you please come back to Cloverleaf Cottage?" Rose asked politely.

Mistress Lily smiled so warmly at Rose that Poppy felt her old jealousy flaring up again. "I'd like to," their teacher said, smoothing the skirt of her blue satin gown. "But I don't work there anymore." Then her voice perked up. "Where are my manners? Kell is in town, but I don't think he'll mind if we go inside. I'm staying on the other side of the lake, but we're meeting here for dinner."

Ruby joined the other two ponies, who were nibbling ferns at the back of the house, while Mistress Lily led Poppy and Rose into the cozy living room. "Kell should be back soon," Mistress Lily said. Humming to herself, she went to put on the kettle for tea.

While Mistress Lily was in the kitchen, Poppy leaned toward Rose. "Don't you think she's acting strange?"

Rose nodded. "I do. And if she's decided not to teach anymore, why didn't she tell anyone till now?"

"It's almost like she's under an *enchantment*," said Poppy.

Rose's eyes widened. "I never thought of that!"

"If she is," said Poppy, "how do we break it?"

"We could tell her about our fashion show," Rose suggested. "If she realizes what she's missing, maybe she'll come to her senses."

"Doesn't hurt to try," Poppy said. But she doubted it would work.

"Sh," whispered Rose. "She's coming back."

Mistress Lily passed around cups of tea and a plate of fancy frosted cupcakes. "It was certainly nice of you to come and visit," she said. "I've told Kell so much about you."

Rose began to talk about their gowns and their plans for the fashion show. Poppy could tell that she was trying to make the show sound exciting, but Mistress Lily seemed to care as little about modeling as Poppy did.

Her teacher listened, but she didn't change her mind about returning.

Poppy soon grew bored with fashion talk. "I think I'll go for a walk in town," she said. If she ran into Kell, perhaps she could speak to him about Mistress Lily. Maybe *he* could convince her to return to Cloverleaf Cottage.

As Poppy started along the road to town, a white horse trotted by. He was strong and sleek and tall enough for the tallest human. What a handsome horse, she thought. It was a bit odd that no one was riding him, though. Then Poppy did a double take. The stallion's hooves faced backward! In seconds, he'd disappeared around the bend.

Poppy had read about white horses with strange hooves in her water fairies book. But before she could think much about it, a shout came from behind her. She turned and saw a handsome male fairy with long blond hair

and beautiful blue-green eyes. Just looking at him, a funny feeling came over Poppy and she forgot all about the white horse!

8

Kell

"Welcome!" the male fairy called out. "You must be Poppy. Lily's told me all about her students. I've half expected some of you to show up!"

"You're Kell!" Poppy exclaimed. "I was hoping I'd find you."

Kell lifted an eyebrow. "Really?" He fell into step with her as they walked back to his house. "It's wonderful that you came to visit

Lily. How long do you plan to stay?"

"Rose and I need to return tomorrow," said Poppy. "The two of us didn't actually come to visit. We didn't even know where to find Mistress Lily until we spoke to someone at the Primrose Hotel. We want her to come back with us."

"I see," said Kell. He kicked a stone. It skittered across the road.

"She never told anyone she wasn't coming back," Poppy continued. "It's not like her. We wonder if she could be under some kind of enchantment."

A frown flitted across Kell's face. But then he smiled again. "I can see how you might think that. But *I* think she's choosing to stay here because that's what she honestly wants."

"Maybe," Poppy said unhappily. Changing the subject, Kell asked about the journey from Cloverleaf Cottage, and they chatted about that the rest of the way back.

Mistress Lily and Rose had fixed dinner while Poppy was gone. After everyone ate, Kell sang. His voice was so beautiful it made Poppy's heart ache. She wondered if Mistress Lily had fallen in love with him. If so, Poppy could certainly see why. "Sing more," she begged when Kell stopped.

But he shook his head. "I feel like dancing," he said. "Lily, would you be so kind as to—"

"Yes, of course," she said before he could finish. She sat down behind a golden harp and began to pick out a lively tune.

Kell's eyes twinkled as he walked up to Poppy. "May I?" he asked, offering his arm.

"Certainly," said Poppy. She was delighted that Kell had asked *her* first, instead of Rose.

He took turns whirling Poppy and Rose around the room. He really was the most enchanting male fairy Poppy had ever met.

Unfortunately, all too soon it was time for bed.

Poppy and Rose settled comfortably in the blossoms of a purple foxglove between the house and the lake. Mistress Lily joined them for the night. "Did you enjoy yourselves?" she asked. "Isn't Kell a great dancer?"

"The best," Poppy agreed.

Rose sighed dreamily. "He's *so* handsome. And I could have listened to him sing all night."

Her words, especially the way she said them, troubled Poppy—but not because of jealousy. She remembered how *she'd* felt just meeting Kell, and when he sang, and when they danced. What if she was right about Mistress Lily being under an enchantment? And what if *Kell* was responsible? Could he be trying to enchant Poppy and Rose, too?

But that was crazy, thought Poppy. Kell

wouldn't do that. He was too nice! She yawned. She was too tired to think properly, that was all. Everything would make better sense in the morning.

Before she drifted off to sleep, Poppy struggled to recall what she'd read about white horses with backward hooves. Weren't they the shape-shifting form that *kelpies* sometimes took? It flitted through her mind that kelpies were known for their fierce tempers. But in the next instant the thought faded and all she could think about was how much fun it had been to dance with Kell and how well he sang.

Early the next morning, Poppy woke to shouts. Mistress Lily and Kell were standing near the house. They appeared to be having an argument. Moments later, Mistress Lily ran inside the house, slamming the door behind her. Kell stalked down to the lake.

Poppy pretended to be asleep as he passed by. Then she heard the wild stamping of a horse's hooves. Nearby, the three winged ponies whinnied nervously. Poppy opened her eyes. Kell had disappeared. In his place stood a white horse with a flowing blond mane and *backward hooves*.

Poppy gasped. Snorting angrily, the horse threw back its head and let out a high-pitched scream. "Wake up, Rose!" Poppy cried. "Kell is a *kelpie*!

Rose sat up. "What's going on?" she asked, rubbing the sleep from her eyes.

Before Poppy could reply, the white horse lowered his head. He glanced toward the house and pawed the ground. Poppy didn't like the wild look in his eyes. Suddenly, he charged across the lawn as if he meant to crash through the door.

"Stop!" cried Poppy. The foxglove she

and Rose were nestled in was directly in the horse's path. They would be trampled under his hooves!

9

Buzz!

Quickly, Poppy shape-shifted into a fly. She flew at the horse and buzzed past his eyes. Flicking his head from side to side, he tried to get rid of Poppy. As she had hoped, he veered from the foxglove. She kept buzzing around him until, gradually, he slowed to a stop.

Mistress Lily rushed out of the house.

"What's going on?" she cried. And she didn't sound enchanted at all!

The stallion's back slumped, and he dropped his head in shame. Then Kell and

Poppy both shape-shifted into their fairy selves.

Rose flew to Poppy at once. "Are you all right?" she asked.

Poppy nodded.

Rose glared at Kell. "You almost trampled us!"

Kell's eyes widened. "But I—"

"Please be quiet," Mistress Lily said firmly. "Now is not the time for excuses."

Rose gave Poppy a look of admiration. "That was some fast thinking you did."

"Thanks," said Poppy. Rose's praise made her feel ashamed for all the times she'd felt jealous.

"What you did was very dangerous, Poppy," Mistress Lily scolded. Then her voice softened. "But it was also very brave." She hugged Poppy.

Her teacher's words and hug made Poppy glow.

Kell shifted from one foot to the other. "I'm sorry I lost my temper," he said. "I don't expect any of you to forgive me."

He seemed so forlorn that pity tugged at Poppy's heart. "Well, maybe—," she started to say.

But Rose interrupted. "You're right not to expect forgiveness," she said coldly.

"We'll start back to Cloverleaf Cottage in an hour," Mistress Lily said, "right after breakfast." She motioned to Kell, and he followed her quietly into the house.

Poppy wondered what Mistress Lily would say to him. Kell's apology had *sounded* sincere. But what would happen the next time he became angry?

Rose leaned against the foxglove's stem. "When did you know that Kell was a kelpie?" she asked.

Poppy explained about the white horse with the backward hooves that she had seen in town the previous day. "I just wish I'd realized he was Kell sooner." How could she have missed the clues? Kelpies were known for their charm—*and* for their musical talents. But perhaps she'd been under a bit of an enchantment herself!

"I'm just glad you figured it out when you did," said Rose. She paused. "You know, sometimes I'm jealous of you."

"Really?" said Poppy. "Why?"

"Well, for one thing, you can shape-shift," said Rose. "I wish I could do that. You're brave, too, just like Mistress Lily said; and you're funny."

"But you're so . . . so *elegant*," said Poppy. "You're good at everything you do. And you're a much better teacher than Mistress Petunia!"

"Why, thank you," said Rose.

"You're welcome." Poppy smiled. This was

a surprise! From now on, whenever she felt jealous of Rose, she would try to remember that Rose was also jealous of *her*.

There was a hazelnut cake topped with honeycomb and blackberry sauce for breakfast. Kell was silent all through the meal. Finally he went outside to stand by the lake. Poppy felt even more sorry for him now that Mistress Lily would be returning to Cloverleaf Cottage. She licked the honey off her fingers and flew outside.

Poppy fluttered up to Kell. "Are you in love with Mistress Lily?" she asked softly.

He nodded.

"Did you put an enchantment on her? Is that why she didn't return to Cloverleaf Cottage when she was supposed to?"

Kell sighed. "I didn't mean for it to happen. I know the effect that my singing and my . . . my *charm* can have." He hung his head. "The thing is, I did nothing to *stop* her enchantment—until this morning, that is."

"This morning?" Poppy repeated.

"Yes. I wanted her to stay here. But I saw how much you missed her. I needed to know if she *really* wanted to stay." Kell paused. "So this morning I deliberately broke the enchantment."

Poppy wondered if whatever he'd done had also broken her own enchantment so she could think more clearly.

"Then what happened?" asked Poppy.

Kell shrugged. "Lily was confused at first, and then she grew upset. She said she loved teaching and had to go back to Cloverleaf Cottage right away." He gazed out at the lake. "It wasn't at all what I'd hoped she'd say."

"And that's when you lost your temper," said Poppy.

Kell looked at her sadly. "I'm sorry. I honestly didn't remember where you were sleeping. I shudder to think that I could have hurt you and Rose."

Poppy thought about her own feelings of jealousy—and anger—toward Rose. Controlling strong emotions wasn't easy.

"I'll miss Lily," said Kell. "But I was wrong to try and keep her here." He paused. "She did say she might come and visit me on her next holiday."

Poppy smiled. "She must like you if she

still wants to see you."

"Do you think so?" Kell asked, sounding hopeful.

"I do," said Poppy. Then she gave him a hug.

10

The Return

Poppy, Rose, and Mistress Lily mounted their ponies and flew home. When they entered Cloverleaf Cottage, Mistress Petunia hurried to meet them. Frowning, she began to grumble. "It's about time you—"

"How wonderful to see you!" interrupted Mistress Lily. She gave Mistress Petunia a great big hug. "I'm sorry to return so late—

and even sorrier for the worry I caused. I'll give you a full explanation. I'm just so glad you were here to look after my students while I was away."

"Oh . . . well . . . I . . ." Looking flustered, Mistress Petunia fanned her wings. "It was nothing, really." Then she smiled. "I'm happy you're back." Now Mistress Petunia could finally go on her vacation, thought Poppy.

Moments later, there were shouts of hello as the rest of the junior fairies zipped down from the balcony.

"We missed you, Mistress Lily," Violet said shyly.

Daisy glanced at Poppy. "*All* of you," she added.

"And I missed you, too," Mistress Lily replied.

"Run along, everyone," said Mistress Petunia. "We'll have lunch soon." She slipped her arm through Mistress Lily's and steered her away from the junior fairies. Poppy imagined the two teachers would have lots to talk about. So would she and Daisy.

"Let's go outside," Marigold suggested. "Then Poppy and Rose can tell us everything that happened."

"Yes, let's!" cried Holly.

Poppy and Daisy held hands as, together again at last, the eight fairies fluttered out

the door and over the lawn. They settled onto the jeweled bridge. Poppy and Daisy sat cross-legged next to each other. So did Rose and Marigold. But Violet and the triplets took off their shoes. They sat on the banks of the stream and dipped their toes in the water.

Heather twisted her head to look at Poppy and Rose. "So why didn't Mistress Lily return when she was supposed to?" she asked.

Poppy shrugged and smiled. "You were right. Mistress Lily was swept off her feet by a handsome male fairy."

The sisters squealed and giggled.

Looking at Poppy, Rose rolled her eyes.

Poppy grinned back at her. Rose was okay, really—*more* than okay. Poppy was glad she could see that now. She waited a few seconds for the triplets to calm down. Then she and Rose told them all about Kell.

Whimsical ___ ___ ait at
Mistress Lily's Fairy School!

Poppy and the Vanishing Fairy

Rose and the Delicious Secret

HarperCollins*Children's*Books   www.harpercollinschildrens.com